INVISIBLE LIZARD

Kurt Cyrus and Illustrated by Andy Atkins

PUBLISHED BY SLEEPING BEAR PRESS

Sleeping Bear Press™

2395 South Huron Parkway, Suite 200, Ann Arbor, MI 48104
www.sleepingbearpress.com
© Sleeping Bear Press

Printed and bound in China.
10 9 8 7 6 5 4 3 2 1

Library of Congress Cataloging-in-Publication Data
Names: Cyrus, Kurt, author. | Atkins, Andy, 1958- illustrator.
Title: Invisible lizard / written by Kurt Cyrus ; illustrated by Andy Atkins.
Description: Ann Arbor, MI : Sleeping Bear Press, [2017] | Summary:
Napoleon the chameleon tries to make friends with animals that
live near him in the jungle, but has a hard time being seen.
Identifiers: LCCN 2017002845 | ISBN 9781585363780 (hard cover)
Subjects: | CYAC: Chameleons—Fiction. | Friendship—Fiction. |
Jungles—Fiction. Classification: LCC PZ7.C9973 Inv 2017 | DDC [E]—dc23
LC record available at https://lccn.loc.gov/2017002845

Once upon a spiffy limb,
there lived a little chameleon named Napoleon.

Napoleon was a colorful guy.

In fact, he was every bit as spiffy as the limb he lived on.

And that was a problem.

Napoleon blended in so well
that he was nearly invisible.

"Hello, Polly," said the lizard. "Nice feathers."

"**Squawk!**" screamed the parrot.

"That tree can *talk*!"

"Yo, Mike!" said the lizard. "You're really swinging today."
"*Eek!*" went the monkey. "*Eee! Ahh! Ooh!*"
"Drat," said Napoleon.

No one ever saw him, even when he waved his arms.

Which took him twenty minutes to do.

Chameleons move very, very slowly.

Everyone wants to be noticed.
So Napoleon flashed his flashiest colors
and sashayed up and down the spiffy limb.

Each sashay took about an hour.
"Hey, look at me!" he said.

But did anyone look?

He wove a wicker welcome mat.

It took a week.

No one saw it.

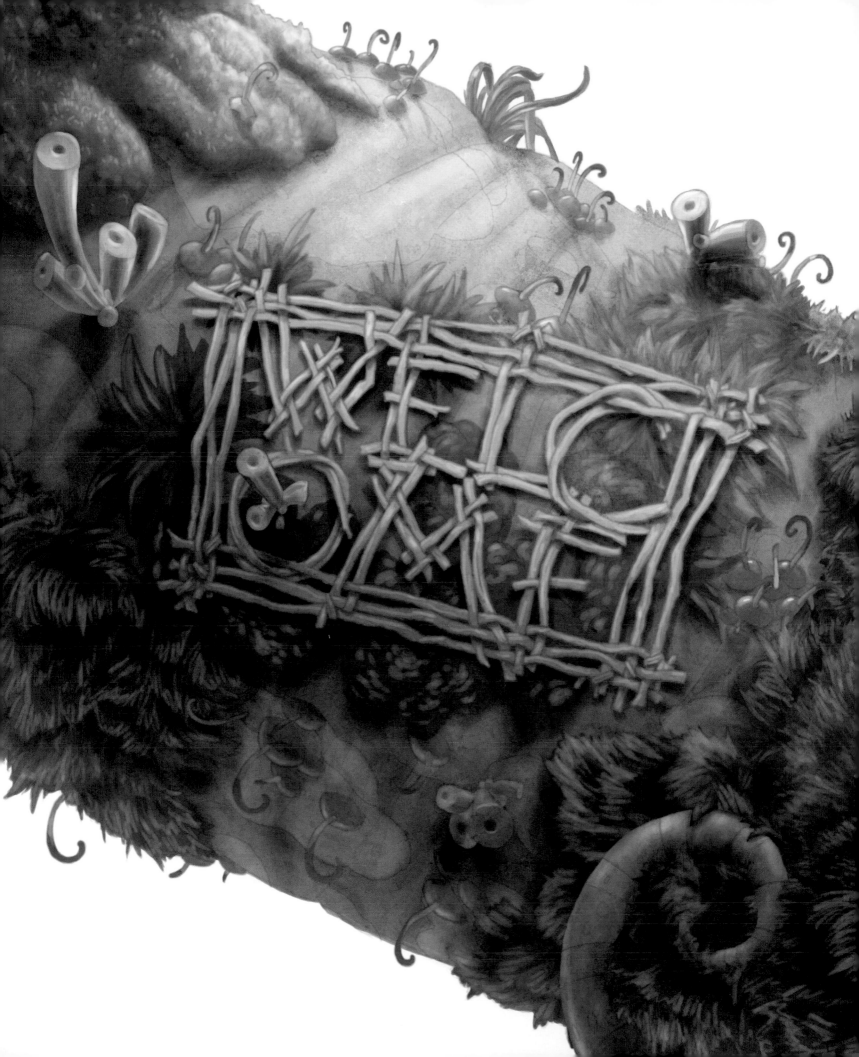

He made a trumpet flower birdbath.
"Hey, Polly! Are you thirsty?"

No Polly.

"Look at me! Funny face! Funny face!"

Nothing.

The lizard turned purple, and his eyes burned red.
"Phooey!"

He had tried to be friendly. He had tried to be flashy.
He had tried to be funny and fun.

"There is one more thing I haven't tried. . . ." he said.

He stood on his head.

Around daybreak, Napoleon began to slip.

There are two things a chameleon can do very fast.
Falling is one. . . .

Flicking his tongue is the other.

Suddenly, everyone saw him.

"**Squawk!**" said Polly.
"Who is that remarkable creature?
Check out those colors!"

"**Ooh!**" said Mike.
"Now *that's* swinging!"

"Cuh you heb be ub?" said Napoleon.

The parrot and the monkey were delighted with their spiffy new friend.
They began visiting Napoleon's limb every day.
The three of them played King of the Tree.
They played Red-Lizard Green-Lizard.

But mostly they played hide-and-seek.
Look very carefully.
Maybe you'll spot them up there
among the ferns and the fungus. . . .

But probably not.